Martin Waddell has written many books for children of all ages. He also writes under the pen-name of Catherine Sefton. He has won a number of awards including the Smarties Prize twice, The Kurt Maschler Award and was a runner-up for the *Guardian* Children's Fiction Prize. He now lives by the sea in Northern Ireland with his wife, three sons and their dog, Bessie.

MARTIN WADDELL

Class Three and the Beanstalk

Illustrated by Toni Goffe

PUFFIN BOOKS

PUFFIN BOOKS

Published by the Penguin Group
Penguin Books Ltd, 27 Wrights Lane, London W8 5TZ, England
Penguin Putnam Inc., 375 Hudson Street, New York,
New York 10014, USA
Penguin Books Australia Ltd, Ringwood, Victoria, Australia
Penguin Books Canada Ltd, 10 Alcorn Avenue, Toronto,
Ontario, Canada M4V 3B2
Penguin Books (NZ) Ltd, Private Bag 102902, NSMC,
Auckland, New Zealand

On the World Wide Web at: www.penguin.com

Penguin Books Ltd, Registered Offices: Harmondsworth,
Middlesex, England

First published as a Blackie Bear by Blackie and Son Limited 1988
Published in Puffin Books 1990
13

Text copyright © Martin Waddell, 1988
Illustrations copyright © Toni Goffe, 1988
All rights reserved

Made and printed in England by Clays Ltd, St Ives plc

British Library Cataloguing in Publication Data
A CIP catalogue record for this book is available from
the British Library

ISBN 0-140-32737-1

CONTENTS

CONTENTS

Class Three
and the Beanstalk

For Stephen

'The window ledge in our classroom is all filled up with big bags!' Alice said. 'Come and see!'

Max and Kit raced down the corridor to Class Three.

'Sandbags!' said Kit.

'Those aren't sandbags,' said Alice. 'They're growbags. You

9

plant things in them and make them grow.'

'We could plant Max,' said Kit.

Then Kit tried to plant Max and Max tried to plant Kit. One of the growbags burst and there was earth all over the place.

That's when Miss Chew the Class Three teacher walked in.

Max and Kit were well and truly CHEWED. They had to brush up the mess, and put the earth they had brushed up back in the growbag. Then they put the growbag with all the other growbags on the window ledge, where they could catch the sun.

'We are going to grow flowers and green things in them,' said Miss Chew. 'Class Three will be just like a garden!'

'Where will we get the seeds from, Miss?' Alice asked.

'You can all bring in your own special favourites,' said Miss Chew.

Class Three spent the rest of the day talking about the growbags and the seeds they were going to bring. Miss Chew wrote up a list of their ideas on the blackboard.

'Bring your seeds to school on Monday!' said Miss Chew.

On Monday, everyone brought seeds in lunch boxes

and bags and envelopes. Soon
there were seeds all over the
place. Pansies and cornflowers
and rosemary and cress and
peas and lettuce and radishes
and forget-me-nots and
marigolds and sweetpeas and
beans.

Miss Chew picked up one of the packets. 'Jackson's Giant Beans,' she said. 'Who brought these?'

Nobody seemed to know.

Class Three kept checking the growbags all day, but nothing happened.

'Wait and watch,' said Miss

Chew. 'Seeds need a bit of time
to grow, you know.'

Nothing much happened for a
couple of days.

Then, on Thursday morning,
Class Three couldn't get into
their classroom. The door was
jammed.

They pushed and they pushed
and they pushed.

Alice organized a charge, but the door wouldn't open.

Miss Chew pushed and pushed and pushed. The door wouldn't open.

Miss Chew went and fetched Mr Stevens the caretaker, and he pushed and pushed and pushed. The door still wouldn't open.

Then they called the teachers from the other classrooms and they all pushed and pushed and pushed. There was a line of teachers outside Class Three's door, all pushing as hard as they could push, but ...

... SOMETHING was pushing the other way.

The something won.

The door creaked and groaned and...

'Look out!' cried Alice.

'Oh no!' wailed Kit.

'It's g-o-i-n-g!' yelled Max.

C-R-E-A-K! The door frame began to twist and C-R-A-S-H! The door burst off its hinges and

17

went flying down the hall. A great big leafy thing shot out of the classroom like a spring uncoiling.

WOOOOOOOOOOOOOOOOSH!

All the teachers were bowled over.

'It's gi-normous!' shouted Kit.

'What is it?' gasped Max.

'It's our beanstalk!' said Alice.

The beanstalk shot halfway down the hall, with all the teachers clinging onto it, hanging from the leaves and branches. It was big and green and soft and leafy, and it swished into everything.

Class Three's classroom was filled to bursting with beanstalk,

and so was the hall, as far as
the Reception door. Everybody
climbed into Class Three's room
to look at the beanstalk. It was
so big that some of the little ones
disappeared under the leaves
and couldn't be seen at all.

'It's BIG!' said Kit.

'The BIGGEST beanstalk I've
ever seen!' breathed Max.

'Three cheers for our
beanstalk!' cried Alice, and
everybody gave three cheers
except the teachers, who were
still trying to fight their way out
of it.

Tap-tap-tap. The leaves of
the beanstalk knocked against
Miss Grimthorpe's office door,

the one with HEADMISTRESS
written on it in big white letters.

Miss Grimthorpe opened the
door.

WOOOOOOOOOOOOOSH!
went the beanstalk, and all at
once Miss Grimthorpe's room
was full of beanstalk, and Miss
Grimthorpe was being
beanstalked out of it, through
the window and into the
playground.

'It's got Miss Grimthorpe!'
shouted Kit, who had climbed
up as high on the beanstalk as
he could, so that he could see
what was happening as the
beanstalk whooshed about the
school.

'Now it's growing into the kitchens!' cried Kit, as the beanstalk whooshed into the school kitchens and sent the soup flying. Then it knocked over the pots and the pans and the plates and the dishwasher and the dinner ladies. They all landed in a heap on the floor.

Then WHOOSH went the beanstalk again, right into the Gym.

'It's climbing up the ropes and round the ceiling!' cried Kit.

The beanstalk WHOOSHED through the skylight and out onto the roof and down the windows into the playground, where it tangled itself around the climbing frame and caught onto the goal posts and scared the cat, who'd been sunning herself in the penalty area.

'Everybody out of the school!' cried Miss Grimthorpe,

unscrambling herself from the beanstalk.

Everybody started to poke and climb and cling and clamber and squeeze to get out through the tiny spaces where the beanstalk wasn't, because the beanstalk almost filled the doors and windows.

'Close the school gates!' cried Miss Grimthorpe.

Alice and Max ran and closed them, just in time to stop the beanstalk whooshing down the road, and covering all the houses.

'It's the Biggest Beanstalk in the World!' said Kit, and he Tarzan-swung off it and rolled

down a leaf to land on the
ground.

'We're all going to be
FAMOUS!' cried Max.

One moment the Class Three
Beanstalk was coiling around
the playground, finding new
things to grow over, including

cars and bicycles and people,
with most of the school covered
up in it. The next moment it
gave a shiver and ...

'H-e-l-p!' cried Miss Chew, as
the leaf she was climbing off
twitched upward.

'Got you!' cried Kit. He
reached out to grab Miss Chew's
jacket and ...

WHOOOOSH!

The beanstalk shot off ...
and up and up and up and
up ...

Till the top of it disappeared
through the clouds.

Miss Chew and Kit shot up
with it.

'To the rescue!' cried Alice

bravely and Alice and Class
Three dived onto the beanstalk.

'HOLD THAT BEANSTALK
DOWN!' cried Miss
Grimthorpe. She didn't want the
World's Biggest Beanstalk to
escape from her school.

All the teachers and all the
children (except Class Three)
and all the dinner ladies and all
the neighbours who had climbed
over the school fence to help,
tried to hold the beanstalk down
but the beanstalk wouldn't stop.

Up and up and up and up it
went.

And up went Class Three with
it!

Class Three and Miss Chew

went up because they were on the beanstalk.

The others didn't, because they were on the ground, trying to tie the beanstalk down with ropes and chains.

But...

WHOOOOOOSH went the beanstalk, and children and teachers and neighbours and ropes and stones and chains were all swept aside.

'H-e-l-p, oh help!' cried Miss Chew.

'Hang on tight!' yelled Kit.

'We're coming to rescue you!' shouted Alice.

Miss Chew and Kit and the rest of Class Three shot up

through the clouds and out the
other side... which wasn't like a
cloud at all.

It was like this:

'VERONICA?' said a very big voice. 'VERONICA! THERE'S ANOTHER BEANSTALK JUST COME UP!'

'WHERE, HAROLD?' said another very big voice.

'RIGHT AMONG THE ROSES!' said Harold.

CLUMP. CLUMP. CLUMP.

A pair of huge green wellies came clumping towards the beanstalk.

'IT MUST BE JACK! I BET HE HAS RUN OUT OF EGGS AGAIN!' said Harold, who owned the first big voice.

'IT'S NOT JACK!' said Veronica, who owned the second big voice.

'WHO IS IT THEN?' said Harold.

'It's us!' cried Class Three, and Miss Chew.

'WHO?' said Veronica.

And her huge giant's face came down and peered at the leaf Class Three were clinging to.

'US!' yelled Class Three.
'Class Three, High End School!'
'And Miss Chew!' said Miss
Chew in a nervous voice. She'd
gone rather white, but she was
trying to be brave, because she
had her Class to look after.

'DID JACK SEND YOU?'
boomed Veronica.

'We don't even know Jack,'
said Max.

He was the smallest one, so
the rest of Class Three had lifted
him up on their shoulders to talk
to the Giants.

'VERY PLEASED TO MEET
YOU, I'M SURE!' boomed
Veronica.

The beanstalk shook, and

Class Three had to cling on
hard to stop themselves being
blown off.

'You're going to blow us off!'
Max shouted.

'SO SORRY!' boomed
Veronica, and she stepped
back about three miles. Then
she spoke to the other Giant.

'IT'S A SCHOOL TRIP,
HAROLD,' she said.

'HAVE THEY BOOKED?'
boomed Harold.

'No!' cried Class Three.

'Does—does it matter?' said
Miss Chew anxiously.

'NOT A BIT!' boomed
Veronica. 'STEP ONTO MY
HAND! YOUR SCHOOL
TOUR OF GIANT LAND
BEGINS IMMEDIATELY!'

Class Three and Miss Chew
dropped one by one onto
Veronica's huge hand. It was as
big as three rooms. Then
Veronica took them on the tour.

They went into the giant
Castle and saw the big table

and the chairs and the stairs
and the giant beds and the giant
kitchen with the giant pots in it.
  'What about the hen?' said
Alice.

Veronica showed them the hen, and gave everybody an egg.

The eggs were made of gold, and marked: LAID IN GIANT LAND.

'AND THAT CONCLUDES YOUR TOUR OF GIANT LAND!' said Veronica.

'Oh...er...thank you very much!' said Miss Chew.

'How do we get home?' said Class Three.

'DOWN THE BEANSTALK!' said Veronica.

Class Three looked down the beanstalk.

'It's...er...a long way down,' said Miss Chew.

'Isn't there a lift?' said Alice.

'NO LIFT,' said Veronica.

'What about that bucket?' said Alice, pointing at a great big giant bucket in the Giant's garden.

'WHAT ABOUT IT?' said
Veronica.

'If you tied a rope to it, you
could lower us down,' said Alice.

And that is what the Giants
did.

Harold tied the rope to the bucket.

Class Three climbed in.

And Harold and Veronica lowered them all the way
down...
and down...
and down...
and down...
to the bottom of the beanstalk.

When they got to the bottom, Veronica called down: 'CAN WE HAVE OUR BEANSTALK BACK, PLEASE?' and Class Three and Miss Chew and all the other classes and all the other teachers rushed around the school, unwinding the beanstalk and putting it into the bucket.

'The beanstalk's loaded,
Veronica!' cried Alice.

'THANK YOU VERY
MUCH!' boomed Veronica.

Up went the bucket, and Class
Three's beanstalk.

Up...

Up...

Up...

and up through the gap in the
clouds.

'Well, that's that!' said Miss
Chew. 'No more beanstalk!'

'Without our beanstalk,
nobody will ever believe it
happened!' said Miss
Grimthorpe.

'Yes they will!' said Alice.
'We've got our eggs!'

And Class Three showed
everybody the eggs with LAID IN
GIANT LAND stamped on them.
   'Just like Jack's golden eggs,'
said Alice.

'WE WANT TO GO TO GIANT LAND TOO!' cried all the other classes and their teachers.

'Well, I'm afraid you can't,' said Miss Chew. 'We haven't got any more beans, so we can't grow another beanstalk!'

'I think I know where the beans came from though...' said Alice.

FOR ALICE

This is the Small family. Tod and
Martha are the mum and dad
and the three little ones are Jeb
and Sam and Milly. They live
across the street from us, at
Number 8 Coke Lane, three doo
up from the gasworks and a sho
walk from the shops.

53

My name is Tom Grice. I'm in the picture holding Tod Small's ferret. The story is really about the big Small who isn't in the picture because he wouldn't fit.

It all began the day a letter came for Martha.

It was as big as a door, and it took four postmen to deliver it, two at each end.

It said:

> HALLO MUM
> COMING HOME WEDNESDAY
> LOVE AND XXXXXXXXXXXXs
> WILBUR

'Wilbur's coming!' cried Martha, and she danced a jig

54

The Tall Story of Wilbur Small

around the postmen, because she
was so happy.

'Not . . . not *your* Wilbur?' said
the postmen, nervously. 'Wilbur
Small?'

'It is! It is!' cried Martha,
joyfully.

'Cor!' said the four postmen,
and they pedalled away as fast as

their bicycles could carry them.

'Tod! Tod!' cried Martha, when
Tod came back from the Coach

and Horses. 'Wilbur's coming! Our little boy!'

'Crikey!' said Tod, and he puffed his pipe so hard that the smoke came wuffing out of his ears.

'Won't we have fun?' said Martha, happily.

'Won't we *just*!' said Tod, and he went out to his ferret shed to think about it.

Jeb and Sam and Milly ran up and down Coke Lane, telling all the neighbours the news.

'Wilbur's coming!' Jeb shouted.

'Our Wilbur's back!' shouted Sam.

'He'll bring us presents!' said Milly.

Everybody was very pleased.
Mrs Ishaq hung a big banner
across the street. It said:

> WELCOME WILBUR SMALL—
> BUT DO BE CAREFULL!

Mr Ishaq and Shahid put
boards up across the windows of
their shop.

Leroy Simpson sent his pigeons
out with messages to all his
friends, saying:

WARNING: WILBUR SMALL!

Serena Simpson started
stitching blankets together, on
behalf of the Coke Lane Welcome
Wilbur Committee.

Mr Murphy ordered twenty
extra barrels of beer for his pub

the Coach and Horses, and put a
big sign in the window:

> This Wednesday is
> WELCOME HOME WILBUR DAY
> Free beer and sausages!

Mrs Murphy doubled her order
for bacon-flavoured crisps,
because she knew Wilbur liked
them. Then she doubled it again,
and again, and again, because
she knew Wilbur.

Oscar Fine started practising
on his tuba and the Coke Lane
School Band paraded up and
down the car park getting ready
for the WELCOME HOME
WILBUR parade.

Colin Leek was sick.

'What's the matter with you,
Col?' asked his mum.

'It's all the excitement,' Colin
said.

The only house where nothing
happened was Number 3, which is
our house, me and Mum and
Dad.

We'd only just come to live in Coke Lane, so we didn't know what all the fuss was about.

'Who's Wilbur?' said Mum.

'I don't know,' said Dad. 'We'd better get Tom to find out.'

I'm the one who does all the finding out in our family. So I went round the houses, asking people who Wilbur was.

'Wilbur's great!' said Shahid Ishaq.

'Wilbur's smashing!' said Colin Leek.

'There's nobody like Wilbur Small!' said Gary Simpson.

'Where've you come from that you've never heard of Wilbur?' said Oscar Fine.

'We've come from Biggleswood!'
I said.

'You'd think they'd have heard
of Wilbur, even in Biggleswood,
wouldn't you?' said Oscar.

'Imagine not knowing Wilbur!'
said Colin Leek.

'Look out for his feet though!'
said Gary Simpson.

'What about his feet?' I said.

Colin Leek said: 'You'll see!'

Then they all laughed and
started telling each other funny
stories, and then everyone went

down to the timber yard next to the foundry and bought piles and piles of planks, and started to board up their windows.

'What are you boarding up your windows for?' I asked.

'Snores!' they all said.

'What about snores?' I said but nobody would tell me. They were all too busy piling sandbags up against their doors.

'What are you piling sandbags up against your doors for?' I asked.

'Just in case!' they said.

'Can't be too careful with Wilbur,' said Oscar Fine.

'Better safe than sorry, after last time,' said Yasmeen Ishaq.

I went home and told Mum and
Dad what everyone had said.
  'We'd better board up *our*
windows, and sandbag *our* doors,
Dad, just in case!' I told him.

'Why?' said Dad.

'Can't be too careful with Wilbur,' I said. 'Better safe than sorry, after last time.'

'Who is Wilbur, and what happened last time?' Dad said.

'I don't know,' I said. 'But you've got to look out for his feet. And snores!'

'What do you make of it, Mum?' said Dad.

'I don't know,' said Mum. 'Wait and see, Dad.'

That's what we did.

And we *saw*, on Wednesday morning.

I was the first one to see Wilbur, and that is because I was the first one to hear him. I heard:

CLUMP CLUMP CLUMP
CLUMP, CLUMP CLUMP,
CLUMPETY CLUMP and I
looked out of my bedroom
window.

There was this foot.

It was a B-I-G foot—about
eight metres long.

It was in our garden, and there was another one in the garden of Number 7, two doors away.

Attached to the two feet were two legs, one on each foot, and attached to the two legs was a bottom.

It was the biggest bottom in the world. It was covered in green corduroy trousers, and it blotted out the sun and the view of the other houses in Coke Lane and the gasometer that I usually see from my window.

'Mum!' I called. 'Dad!'

'What is it, Tom?' said Mum and Dad.

'I think . . . I think it's Wilbur!' I said.

And it was.

'My roses!' shrieked Dad, looking out of the window. He ran outside and started shouting up at Wilbur.

'Pardon?' said Wilbur, bending down.

Then he picked Dad up, and Dad disappeared. I couldn't see him because of the big bottom. I had to run round Wilbur's foot and crash-scratch through our hedge, and then I saw Dad scolding Wilbur.

Dad was in Wilbur's hand, and he sounded really cross. I thought poor Wilbur was going to cry.

Then Wilbur's mum started in on my dad. She was up on Wilbur's shoulder and was just giving him a kiss when Dad came out shouting about his roses.

'My Wilbur didn't mean any harm, Mr Grice,' she said. 'He's come home to see his old mum, and he stood on your roses by mistake!'

'Just a mistake, Mr Grice,' said Wilbur. 'I'm really sorry.'

Dad was still muttering crossly, but then Mum came out of our house and climbed up on Wilbur's foot and shouted:

'Arthur! Arthur! You stop scolding that boy!' My dad is called Arthur and he did stop scolding Wilbur because he didn't want to upset Mrs Small.

The Smalls are really nice people.

All the rest of the people in Coke Lane came rushing out to see Wilbur.

'My, hasn't he grown!' said Serena Simpson.

'Cold up there, is it, Wilbur?' said Mr Murphy.

'Come on down to the Coach and Horses, Wilbur, for your party,' said Mrs Murphy.

Everybody went down to the Coach and Horses, and everybody jammed into the pub and the back garden and started on the free beer and sausages and the bacon-flavoured crisps.

Except Wilbur.

Wilbur couldn't get in.

He could put his arm inside for crisps, just about, and he could bend down and look through the windows, or speak to them down the chimney (only the soot made his teeth black and tasted funny) but he couldn't get into the party. So in the end the party came out to Wilbur.

CLUMP CLUMP CLUMP
CLUMP, CLUMP CLUMP,
CLUMPETY CLUMP went
Wilbur, as he stepped over the
houses in Coke Lane and made
his way to the park. He lay down
on the football pitch, with his feet
resting on one crossbar, his head
resting on the other and his body

on a great big blanket the Coke
Lane Welcome Wilbur
Committee had made specially
for Wilbur.

Then we had the WELCOME
HOME WILBUR parade.

The parade went right round
Wilbur. Everybody was in it.

First there were the Smalls,
Martha and Tod and Jeb and
Sam and Milly. Martha and Tod
had a big sign with WILBUR IS
OUR BABY on it. Jeb and Sam
and Milly had three little signs
with WILBUR IS OUR BIG
BROTHER on them.

Mr and Mrs Ishaq came next
with a sign which said WILBUR
SHOPS AT ISHAQ'S. Then

came Shahid, Anwar and Yasmeen Ishaq with DO BE CAREFUL WILBUR on their sign.

Leroy Simpson's sign said COKE LANE PIGEON CLUB WELCOMES WILBUR and Gary and Marlene Simpson's said OUR MUM SEWED UP WILBUR'S BLANKET.

Mr Murphy had THE COACH AND HORSES WELCOMES WILBUR! on his sign and Mrs Murphy had TRY OUR WILBUR BURGERS on hers.

The Coke Lane Welcome Wilbur Committee sign said WE LOVE WILBUR XXXX.

Oscar Fine played his tuba and
the Coke Lane School Band
paraded up and down Wilbur's
leg and tickled him.

Colin Leek and his mum hadn't got a sign, because Colin had been sick on it just before he came out of the house, through too much excitement waiting up all night for Wilbur to come.

Last in the parade came my mum and my dad and me. My dad had a sign saying: WELCOME WILBUR BUT WHAT ABOUT MY ROSES? My mum had crossed the last bit out so that the sign just said WELCOME WILBUR. I had a sign saying: WILBUR'S GOT A BIG BOTTOM only I hid it when I was going past his face, in case Wilbur was cross.

It was the B-I-G-G-E-S-T party I've ever been to.

It went on and on and on and on, until the moon came up over the gasworks, and we all had to start putting up Wilbur's tent.

It was a big stripy tent which

81

the Coke Lane Welcome Wilbur Committee had borrowed from a circus. Wilbur lay in the middle, covered by Serena Simpson's blanket and we all helped put the tent up round him. Then we *dinged* and *donged* all the tent pegs in and tied down the ropes and Wilbur was snug and cumfy.

We all went home to bed.

And that was when the trouble started.

SNORE SNORE, SNORE SNORE,

and

SNORE SNORE

and

SNORE SNORE SNORE SNORE!

and

AT-TISH-OOO!

Roofs rattled and TV aerials blew away, up and down the Lane. The gasometer creaked and Leroy's pigeons squawked and the ferrets panicked and all the street lamps flickered.

My mum got ear muffs.

My dad put cotton wool in his
ears.

I hid under the pillow.

We all got to sleep, somehow,
then:

We woke up!
There was soapy water
everywhere.

It was all over our house, in our
clothes and in our cupboards,
washing round the sitting room
and lapping up the kitchen walls,
spilling out into the yard, and
flooding over the fence to next
door.

My mum and dad were floating
round the house, on their bed.

The bed was made of iron, so it soon sank.

My bed was better, because it was made of wood. I hauled Mum and Dad up on to it, all covered in soap.

'What happened?' gasped Mum.

'It's that Wilbur . . .' said Dad.
'. . . Having a wash!' I said.
I was right.
Wilbur was taking his morning
bath in the boating pond, in the
middle of the park. Every time
Wilbur moved, the water rushed
down our street and streamed
around the gasworks.

Dad got very cross and in the end we rowed my bed out of the house and up Coke Lane to the park, to tell Wilbur about it.

We didn't get very far, because every time we got close to Wilbur, he gave another splash, and we were washed right back to our house again.

'Nobody else got wet!' I told Dad.

'They all had sandbags!' said Mum.

'And they all boarded their windows!' I said. 'To keep out the snores.'

'Bah!' said Dad.

He calmed down when the water went away and Martha

and Tod and Jeb and Sam and
Milly took all our wet things up to
the park for Wilbur to dry with a
huge P-U-F-F-F!

And Wilbur got my mum some
flowers. They were.oak trees
really, but Mum said 'Thank you
very much Wilbur!' and didn't
tell him, and we planted them
back in the park when he'd gone.

It was time for Wilbur to go.
'Bye-bye! Bye-bye Wilbur!'
everybody shouted, and Wilbur
kissed his mum and dad and his
little brothers and his sister Milly

and he went CLUMP CLUMP
CLUMP CLUMP, CLUMP
CLUMP, CLUMPETY
CLUMP right out of town, and
over the horizon.

'Come back soon, Wilbur,'
everybody shouted.

92

Then they took away the signs
and the Welcome Wilbur banner
and unboarded their windows
and put away the sandbags and
gave the stripy tent back to the
circus with a note saying:
THANK YOU VERY
MUCH FOR THE
KIND USE OF YOUR
TENT. CAN WE
HAVE IT AGAIN
NEXT TIME,
PLEASE?
Signed:
For and on behalf of the
Coke Lane Welcome
Wilbur Committee
Serena Simpson
(Chairperson).

'Next time?' said my dad.

'Next time Wilbur comes!' I told him.

'Oh no!' groaned my dad.

'Oh yes!' shouted everybody.

READ MORE IN PUFFIN

For children of all ages, Puffin represents quality and variety – the very best in publishing today around the world.

For complete information about books available from Puffin – and Penguin – and how to order them, contact us at the appropriate address below. Please note that for copyright reasons the selection of books varies from country to country.

On the worldwide web: www.penguin.co.uk

In the United Kingdom: Please write to *Dept. EP, Penguin Books Ltd, Bath Road, Harmondsworth, West Drayton, Middlesex UB7 0DA*

In the United States: Please write to *Penguin Putnam inc., P.O. Box 12289, Dept B, Newark, New Jersey 07101-5289* or call 1-800-788-6262.

In Canada: Please write to *Penguin Books Canada Ltd, 10 Alcorn Avenue, Suite 300, Toronto, Ontario M4V 3B2*

In Australia: Please write to *Penguin Books Australia Ltd, P.O. Box 257, Ringwood, Victoria 3134*

In New Zealand: Please write to *Penguin Books (NZ) Ltd, Private Bag 102902, North Shore Mail Centre, Auckland 10*

In India: Please write to *Penguin Books India Pvt Ltd, 11 Panscheel Shopping Centre, Panscheel Park, New Delhi 110 017*

In the Netherlands: Please write to *Penguin Books Netherlands bv, Postbus 3507, NL-1001 AH Amsterdam*

In Germany: Please write to *Penguin Books Deutschland GmbH, Metzlerstrasse 26, 60594 Frankfurt am Main*

In Spain: Please write to *Penguin Books S. A., Bravo Murillo 19, 1° B, 28015 Madrid*

In Italy: Please write to *Penguin Italia s.r.l., Via Felice Casati 20, I-20124 Milano*

In France: Please write to *Penguin France S. A., 17 rue Lejeune, F-31000 Toulouse*

In Japan: Please write to *Penguin Books Japan, Ishikiribashi Building, 2-5-4, Suido, Bunkyo-ku, Tokyo 112*

In South Africa: Please write to *Longman Penguin Southern Africa (Pty) Ltd, Private Bag X08, Bertsham 2013*